Harold
the Helicopter

Based on *The Railway Series* by the Rev. W. Awdry

Illustrations by *Robin Davies*

EGMONT

This is a story about Harold the Helicopter. He thought helicopters were faster than engines because they have propellers instead of wheels. But then Percy challenged him to a race . . .

Percy was delivering trucks of stone to the Harbour. At the Airfield nearby, there was a helicopter buzzing loudly as it waited to land.

"Loud, buzzy thing!" said Percy to his Driver. "I wish it would go and buzz somewhere else!"

The next day, Percy made a delivery to the Airfield He stopped next to the helicopter.

"Hello," said Percy. "My name's Percy. Who are you?"

"I'm Harold," said the helicopter. "With my whirling propeller, I can fly like a bird! Don't you wish you had a propeller, too?"

"No, I like having my wheels on the rails," replied Percy, grumpily.

"You engines are much too slow," Harold continued. "With my propeller, I can go much faster than any of you!"

Percy was cross but before he could reply, Harold flew away.

Percy puffed angrily to the Quarry to pick up his next load of trucks.

"Hello, Percy," said Toby. "You look cross. What's the matter?"

Percy told Toby what Harold had said about helicopters being faster than engines.

"I'll show him he's wrong!" said Percy, firmly.

As Percy puffed back to the Harbour, he heard a familiar buzzing noise ahead of him.

"Look, Percy," said his Driver. "There's Harold. Let's race him! Then he'll see who's fastest!"

"Yes, we'll show him wheels are better than those funny whirling arms!" said Percy and he rushed after Harold.

Harold heard Percy speeding up behind him. He realised Percy was racing him to the Harbour.

"You'll never beat me!" he said, proudly. "I will have landed at the Airfield before you can stop at the Harbour Wharf!"

"Don't listen to him," said Percy's Driver. "We can win this!"

The race was on! Harold thought a little engine pulling heavy trucks full of stone could never beat him. But suddenly, he saw that Percy was drawing level with him.

A few minutes later Percy's Driver shouted, "We're in the lead, Percy!"

Percy was having the time of his life, racing along faster than he had ever gone before.

"Peep! Peep! Goodbye, Harold!" he shouted as he raced ahead.

Harold looked down in surprise. He couldn't believe Percy was beating him. Harold charged after him.

Percy's Fireman was shovelling coal into the furnace as fast as he could. He wiped a cloth across his hot face.

"Phew!" he said. "This is hard work. I hope we do beat Harold!"

Then he heard the signal that warned them the Harbour Wharf was nearby.

"Nearly there!" cried Percy's Driver. "I hope we've done enough to win!"

Percy braked as he approached the Wharf. He rolled under the main line and halted at the buffers, puffing loudly.

"Did . . . we . . . win?" he said breathlessly.

His Fireman scrambled on to the cab roof and looked at the Airfield. "We've won!" he gasped. "Harold's still looking for a place to land!"

Percy smiled. He had shown Harold that engines are just as fast as helicopters.

Later, Harold looked embarrassed when Percy made a delivery at the Airfield.

Percy's Driver and Fireman sang a song:
Said Harold Helicopter to our Percy,
"You are much too slow!
Your Railway is out of date
And not much use, you know."
But Percy with his stone trucks
Did the trip in record time,
And we beat Harold the Helicopter
On our Old Branch Line!

Harold smiled at Percy as he flew over him. "You showed me that you can go even faster than me," he said. "I guess wheels are as good as a propeller after all!"

Percy smiled happily. What fun it had been racing against Harold. He couldn't wait to get back to the engine shed and tell the others all about it.

Thomas Story Library

 Thomas

 Edward

 Henry

 Gordon

 James

 Percy

Toby

 Emily

 Alfie

 Annie and Clarabel

 'Arry and Bert

 Arthur

 Bertie

 Bill and Ben

Peep!
Peep!

 BoCo

 Bulgy

 Charlie

 Cranky

 Daisy

 Dennis

 Diesel

 Donald and Douglas

Duck

Duncan

The Fat
Controller

Fergus

Freddie

George

Harold

Hector

Hiro

Jack

Jeremy

Kevin

Mighty Mac

Murdoch

Oliver

Peter Sam

Rocky

Rosie

Rusty

Salty

Sir Handel

Skarloey

Spencer

Stepney

Terence

Trevor

Troublesome
Trucks

Victor